From the casebook of

J. P. LANDERS,
MASTER DETECTIVE

SOLVE A
MYSTERY

BOOK 3

By Marian Lee
Illustrations by Steven Crombie

CHILDRENS PRESS, CHICAGO

Library of Congress Cataloging in Publication Data

Lee, Marian
  Solve a mystery.

  (From the casebook of J.P. Landers, master detective)
  Summary: J.P. Landers, boy detective, solves neighborhood mini-mysteries but the reader has an opportunity
to solve the cases first.
  [1. Mystery and detective stories] I. Crombie, Steven,
ill. II. Title. III. Series.
PZ7.L5137So 1982   [Fic]   82-9712
ISBN 0-516-01993-7 (v. 3)

TABLE OF CONTENTS

INTRODUCTION

Jeffrey P. Landers, J.P. to his friends, is already a Master Detective. He has an office in the garage and people come from all corners of the neighborhood to seek his help. J.P. has solved every case.

The cases in this book are taken directly from Jeffrey's files. Some cases involve Jamie Danton, the madcap riddler and Margot Monroe, the master storyteller. Neither one can stump the master detective.

Read each case carefully and look for the hidden clues. Can you match wits with J.P., the famous detective? Once you have solved the case then see if you can break J.P.'s code at the end of the book. Did you spot the one clue that solved the mystery?

MINI MYSTERY #1

BIRDS OF A FEATHER

Jeffrey P. Landers, Master Detective, was in the front yard watering his mother's flowers.

"Hi, J.P.," called Peter Winslow, walking across the lawn. With him was a tall boy carrying binoculars. "This is my friend Rodney Thurston."

"Hi, Rodney," said J.P. He turned the water off and dropped the hose on the grass. "Where are you guys going?"

"We're off to the park," said Peter. "Rodney is an expert bird-watcher. For a dollar he is going to teach me how to spot rare birds."

"Yes," said Rodney. "I've seen many interesting birds in the park. I've seen a red-throated humming bird, a mocking bird, a blue jay, and yesterday, right after lunch, I saw a great horned owl. His hooting was almost ear shattering."

J.P. gave Rodney a strange look and then he turned to Peter. "I wouldn't give him anything," he said. "He is putting you on. He doesn't know anything about birds."

"Are you sure?" asked Peter.

"Yes," said J.P., and he explained why.

Can you find Rodney's mistake? Don't spend all day and all night looking for the clue.

Did you match wits with the famous detective? Turn to page 42 and find out.

MINI MYSTERY #2

CHORES GALORE

J.P. was sitting in his office in the garage. He had a new mystery from the library. He was halfway through the second chapter when the garage door opened and in bounded Jamie Danton.

"Hi, J.P.," said Jamie. "I hope you're not too busy to hear another riddle."

"I guess not," said J.P., putting down his book and stretching his arms. "My eyes need a rest anyway."

"Okay," said Jamie, as he pulled up a lawn chair. "This morning my mother gave me ten chores to do. She said I had to have them all done by dinner time."

"Wow," exclaimed J.P. "That's a lot of work. Are you done?"

"No," said Jamie. "I finished all but six. How many do I have left to do?"

"What a silly riddler you are," said J.P. "You forgot math was my best subject." J.P. told Jamie the answer.

Disappointed, Jamie got up to leave. "I'll be back," he promised as he walked out the door.

"No doubt you will," said J.P., as he picked up his book again.

Do you know the answer? Find the one-word clue but be careful and don't stumble over it.

Did you match wits with the famous detective? Turn to page 42 and find out.

MINI MYSTERY #3

TOPSY TURVY

J.P. hurried up the steps of the Madison public library. It was hot outside so sitting in an air-conditioned library seemed like a cool idea. Miss Emily Snodgrass, the librarian, was seated behind the checkout desk. The reading tables were half filled with summer school students from the local college.

"Hello, Jeffrey," whispered Miss Emily. She didn't want to disturb the students.

"Hi," said J.P., as he dropped his book in the book return slot. He took a detective magazine off the rack and sat down at one of the reading tables. A redheaded boy, sitting across from him, was reading a large book. J.P. had to turn his head almost upside down to read the title. That's strange, thought J.P.

Suddenly the silence was broken by two policemen rushing into the library. Miss Emily jumped up in alarm.

"Good morning, officers," she said. "Is something wrong?"

"We're looking for a shoplifter," said one of the policemen. "He was last seen running in here."

"You must be mistaken," said Miss Emily. "I didn't see anyone come in except Jeffrey P. Landers. And he's certainly not a thief. He's a Master Detective."

"The thief has red hair," said the policeman, looking suspiciously at the boy across from J.P.

The boy squirmed in his chair. "I didn't do anything," he said. "I've been right here reading for the past hour."

"That's not true," said J.P. "This boy is lying. He hasn't been reading at all."

The redheaded boy bolted out of his chair and ran for the door but the policemen grabbed him. They took him away in handcuffs.

"That was brilliant, Jeffrey," cried Miss Emily. "But how did you know the boy was lying? He was here when you got to the library."

"He made one fatal mistake," said J.P., and he went on to explain why. Then he went back to reading his detective magazine.

What was the boy's mistake? Turn up the right clue and close this case pronto.

Did you match wits with the famous detective?
Turn to page 43 and find out.

MINI MYSTERY #4

THE CHALK DRAWING PHANTOM

J.P. walked into his classroom. His desk was in the last row. Just as he was about to sit down he noticed Andy Bartel had his right arm in a cast. The cast ran from his finger tips to his elbow.

"Hey, Andy," said J.P. "What happened?"

"Fell off my skateboard," answered Andy. "My own fault. I was showing off."

"I bet a girl was involved," laughed J.P., as he sat down. "But look at the bright side. Being right-handed you'll get out of doing homework for a while."

Suddenly J.P.'s attention turned to the front of the room. Mrs. Schenk was arguing with Tony Evans.

"I'm surprised at you, Tony," she said. "I would have thought washing blackboards for two months would have cured you of any more chalk drawings." She angrily erased the ugly picture drawn on the blackboard.

"I didn't do it," insisted Tony. "It was Andy Bartel. I saw him drawing on the blackboard before class."

Mrs. Schenk looked up in surprise and stared across the room at Andy. "Andy," she said. "Is this true?"

"No . . . oh no," stammered Andy. "I'd never do that."

"Maybe I can help," said J.P., standing up.

"Oh no," groaned Tony, "Super detective is turning into super fink."

"You deserve it," said J.P. "It's not nice to blame others for your wrong doing. There is no way Andy could have drawn that picture."

"How do you know?" asked Mrs. Schenk.

After Jeff explained, Mrs. Schenk promptly took Tony Evans down to the principal's office once again.

How did J.P. know? Look for the clue and right the terrible wrong in this case.

Did you match wits with the famous detective? Turn to page 43 and find out.

THE CASE OF THE
MYSTERIOUS FIREWORKS

The school lunchroom was a hubbub of activity when Jeffrey P. Landers, Master Detective, entered. He took a seat at the end of a long table filled with other students from his class. Margot Monroe, a master herself at story telling, was just about to begin another tall tale.

"My family travels a lot," boasted Margot. Then she took a big bite of her peanut butter and pickle sandwich.

"How exciting," exclaimed Dawn Leann. "I wish I could travel. The farthest I've been is across town."

"Yes, it's quite an experience," said Margot. "I'll never forget the time we went to the Fourth of July celebration in London, England. Their fireworks were breathtaking. It's hard to describe their beauty."

"I bet it is," said J.P., "because you never saw them."

"What?" cried Margot. "How would you know?"

"Any American would know," said J.P., as he ripped open his lunch bag.

What's wrong with Margot's story? Find the answer and close this case with a bang.

Did you match wits with the famous detective? Turn to page 44 and find out.

THE PET SHOP MYSTERY

J.P. was on his way home from a spy movie at the Strand Theater. It was close to supper time when he turned the corner on Elm Street. In the middle of the block, standing in front of his house, was Jamie Danton, the madcap riddler.

"Hi, J.P.," said Jamie. "I'm glad we bumped into each other."

"I'm not," said J.P. "I'm in a hurry to get home. I'm starved."

"But I have a riddle for you," said Jamie.

"That doesn't surprise me," said J.P. "Well, go ahead, but make it quick."

"Okay," said Jamie, beaming. "Yesterday I walked into Mr. Beetle's Bird and Puppy Shop. Suddenly I was aware of 60 eyes on me and those 60 eyes had 90 feet.

"Sounds spooky," said J.P., "but what's the riddle?"

"The riddle is," said Jamie, "how many birds and puppies does Mr. Beetle have?"

"That's easy," said J.P., and he told Jamie the answer. Then he hurried home to supper.

How many birds and puppies? Add up the facts and find the answer.

Did you match wits with the famous detective? Turn to page 44 and find out.

MINI MYSTERY #7

BIKE HEIST

One morning while J.P. was out riding his bike he decided to stop at Mr. Long's drugstore. He wanted to get some bubble gum. J.P. leaned his bike against the wall of the drugstore and started in the door. He met Anna Benson coming out. She was all dressed up in a long blue skirt and white ruffled blouse.

"Hi, J.P.," said Anna.

"Hi," said J.P. "My you look pretty. Are you going someplace special?"

"Yes," said Anna. "I'm on my way to Ellen Sue's birthday party. I stopped by Mr. Long's to buy blue stockings. Look," she said, raising her long skirt a few inches.

"Stop, stop," yelled David Hamilton, running up behind J.P. His face was red and he looked angry. "I caught you," he yelled in Anna's face. "You stole my bike."

Anna looked shocked. "I did not," she protested.

"I saw you," said David. "Well, I mean I saw somebody wearing blue and white take off on my bike. And look, there it is." He was pointing to a black and yellow boy's bike behind Anna. It was leaning against the wall next to J.P.'s bike.

"I don't know how that got there," said Anna, "but I didn't touch your dumb bike."

"Anna's telling the truth," said J.P. "There's no way she could have ridden your bike." J.P. went on to explain why. David apologized and rode his bike on home.

"Thanks, J.P.," sighed Anna. "It's nice to have a Master Detective around when you need one."

Why couldn't Anna have been the bike thief? Don't look too long for the clue.

Did you match wits with the famous detective? Turn to page 45 and find out.

MINI MYSTERY #8

THE BROWN DOOR

Mrs. Schenk sent J.P. to the school office to pick up some supplies. Outside the office door, J.P. found Mr. Bruna, the janitor, ranting and raving in Italian. Scott Meyers, a tough sixth grader, stood nearby.

"I don't understand kids today," said Mr. Bruna. He turned and gave Scott an angry look. "He comes into my office, so bold this one, and steals my watch right out of my desk."

J.P. thought about Mr. Bruna's office tucked away in the far corner of the basement. His office door was painted brown, just like his name. J.P. is one of the few students ever allowed in the school basement.

"It's not fair picking on me," said Scott. "I always get blamed for everything. Not only have I never been near your brown door, I've never been in the school basement."

"That's not true," said J.P. "You were in the school basement all right. At least once while you were being a sneak thief."

Trapped by the Master Detective, Scott admitted stealing the watch. Just as Mr. Bruna was about to take Scott into the principal's office, Scott turned to J.P. "How did you know? What gave me away?" he asked.

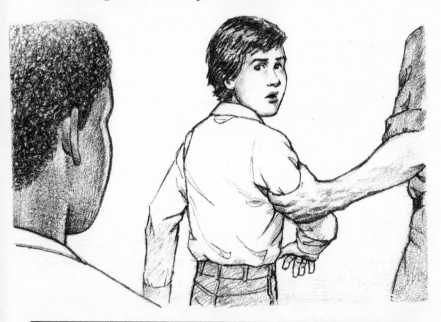

Do you know? Find the right clue and you can shut the door on this case.

Did you match wits with the famous detective?
Turn to page 45 and find out.

MINI MYSTERY #9

THE BALLOON MAN

Jeffrey P. Landers, Master Detective, was sitting on a park bench fanning himself with his detective hat. It was scorching hot and there was not one bit of breeze.

Across the playground two policemen were talking to the park balloon man. Another man, in a white jogging suit, stood a few feet away. J.P. walked over to see what was going on.

"You're quite mistaken," said the balloon man. His face was red and sweaty. "My helium tank is empty. I've been stuck here all morning blowing up my balloons."

"I'm sorry, sir," said one of the police, "but we have an eyewitness, Mr. Jones." He pointed to the man in the jogging suit.

"That's right," said Mr. Jones, stepping forward. "I saw the whole thing. I was jogging past the tennis courts when I noticed one of your balloons floating around in a tree branch. A cute little girl stood below crying. So I climbed the tree to get the balloon. While I was up there I saw you snatch that old lady's purse."

"He's lying," cried J.P., "quick, grab him."

Startled by J.P.'s outburst, Mr. Jones turned and raced off down the jogging path with the two policemen in hot pursuit.

"Thanks," said the balloon man. "You saved me. But how did you know he was lying? It was his word against mine."

How did J.P. know? Look for the hidden clues that knocked the wind out of the jogger's story.

Did you match wits with the famous detective? Turn to page 45 and find out.

MINI MYSTERY #10

BIG FOOT

"Something strange is going on," said Lori Grady, as she walked into J.P.'s office in the garage.

"What do you mean?" asked J.P. He was sitting behind his orange-crate desk typing up his notes.

"It's my garden," said Lori. "There are giant footprints all over my garden."

"Hmmm," said J.P. "That is strange. Let's have a look." He grabbed his detective hat and magnifying glass and followed Lori to her house.

Lori took J.P. to her garden behind the garage. She pointed out the giant footprints in the soft dirt. J.P. took out his magnifying glass and searched for clues.

"Wow," he exclaimed. "These are big and recently made, too. Let's go check the garage."

Lori led the way into the garage. In the back corner behind some boxes, J.P. found an old pair of Mr. Grady's boots. They had fresh mud on the soles.

"This is important evidence," said J.P., as he studied the boots with his magnifying glass. As he looked for more clues, the garage door opened and Greg Grady came in pushing his bike.

"What are you doing?" said Greg, startled to find anyone in the garage.

"Oh, nothing," said Lori. "By the way, have you used these old boots of Dad's?"

"Sure," said Greg smiling. "I used them a while ago when I washed Mom's car. I didn't want my new tennis shoes to get wet."

"Nice try," said J.P., "but I think you're up to your old tricks again. You used these boots to walk through Lori's garden."

Greg started to laugh. Caught again by the super sleuth, he admitted making the footprints. He wanted Lori to think a giant was in her garden.

"I don't understand," said Greg. "What gave me away this time?"

Do you know? Dig out the clues and you'll clean up this case in a hurry.

Did you match wits with the famous detective? Turn to page 46 and find out.

MINI MYSTERY #11

MONEY BY THE DOZEN

One day in late summer, J.P. decided to treat himself to an ice cream cone. A double dip cherry marble delight sounded real yummy. But when J.P. entered the ice cream shop, who did he find sitting at the counter but Jamie Danton.

"Well, well, if it isn't the madcap riddler," said J.P.

"Hi, super sleuth," said Jamie. "Your timing is perfect. I was just thinking about a riddle I heard. Care to give it a shot?"

"Why not?" said J.P. He sat down next to Jamie and ordered his ice cream cone.

"Here it goes," said Jamie, after J.P. got his ice cream. "If there are twelve one dollar bills in a dozen, how many five dollar bills in a dozen?"

"Nothing to it," said J.P., and he told Jamie the answer. Then J.P. took a big lick of his ice cream cone and headed out the door.

Jamie looked sad but only for a moment. He had a super duper banana split to cheer him up. Besides he knew he'd stump the Master—someday.

Can you solve the riddle? Match wits with J.P. and solve this riddle with ease.

Did you match wits with the famous detective?
Turn to page 46 and find out.

MINI MYSTERY #12

MIXED-UP PAPERBOYS

J.P. was the last student out of school. He had stayed behind to help Mrs. Schenk. The playground was deserted but a small crowd had gathered in the parking lot. J.P. hurried over to see what was going on.

In the middle of the crowd was Terry Westlawn. Terry was a seventh grader and paperboy for the Madison *Morning Gazette.*

"This is the boy, all right," said a large man in a mechanic's jumpsuit. He pointed to Terry as Mr. Olson, the vice-principal, watched.

"Are you sure?" asked Mr. Olson. "Terry is one of our best students."

"Course I'm sure," said the man. "It was getting close to dark when I came home from work but I could still see. And I saw this boy stealing hubcaps as he was delivering papers. I saw him put the hubcaps in the newspaper bag."

"Oh dear," said Mr. Olson. "What do you have to say, Terry?"

"I'm innocent," said Terry.

"Terry is telling the truth," said J.P., pushing his way through the crowd. "This man has made a mistake and I can prove it." J.P. went on to explain why Terry was not the newspaper boy that the man saw.

Do you know why Terry was innocent? Look for the clue in the story and you'll be able to clear Terry, too.

Did you match wits with the famous detective? Turn to page 47 and find out.

MINI MYSTERY #13

DOGNAPPING

Jeffrey P. Landers was in his office in the garage. Suddenly the door banged open and Jimmy Franklin rushed in.

"J.P., J.P.," cried Jimmy, "I need your help."

"Sure," said J.P., putting on his detective hat. "What's the problem?"

"It's Snookers, he's gone," said Jimmy.

"I'm sorry," said J.P. "I never take cases involving lost pets. That's the Humane Society's job."

"You don't understand," cried Jimmy. "He's not lost. He's been dognapped."

"Wow," said J.P. "I'll take the case. Now give me the facts." J.P. took out his notebook and pen.

"Yesterday around five, I was playing with Snookers in the backyard," said Jimmy. "Then I went in to get his supper. When I came back out he was gone and a ransom note was tacked to his doghouse."

"What did the note say?" asked J.P.

"I was to leave two dozen chocolate chip cookies near the fountain in the park," said Jimmy.

"Did you do it?" asked J.P.

"Of course," said Jimmy. "I didn't want anything to happen to my Snookers."

"Then what's the problem?" asked J.P. "Didn't you get Snookers back?"

"No," cried Jimmy. "And this morning I found another note but I can't read it. It must be in some kind of foreign language." Jimmy handed J.P. the note.

J.P. took out his magnifying glass and studied the note for a long time. "This looks like the work of Bert the Bully," said J.P. "Bert hates dogs but loves chocolate chip cookies."

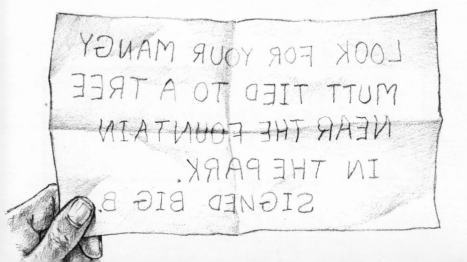

"Oh no," cried Jimmy. "Now I'll never see Snookers again. Bert will never tell me where Snookers is."

"No," said J.P., "but I can. It's right here in the note." J.P. handed Jimmy the note and showed him how to read it.

Jimmy ran off to get Snookers while J.P. went down the block to have a talk with Bert the Bully.

Do you know where Snookers is? Match wits with J.P. and break the code in the note.

Did you match wits with the famous detective?
Turn to page 47 and find out.

MINI MYSTERY #14

THE TIMELESS CLOCK

J.P. knocked on the door at 2310 Spruce Street, home of Bert the Bully. J.P. was not too eager to confront Bert face to face, but he was not going to let him get away with dognapping.

J.P. knocked again. After the third time he knocked, an elderly man opened the door.

"Hello," said the man, leaning on a cane.

"Hello," said J.P., "is Bert home?"

"Yes indeed, come on in," said the elderly man. "I'm Bert's grandfather. Gus is the name. What's yours?"

"Jeffrey P. Landers," said J.P., looking at a large grandfather's clock in the hallway. "My, what a beautiful old clock."

"Thank you," said Gus. "I made that clock myself over fifty years ago. But it stopped dead ten years back. I tried to fix it but my eyes are not good for close work anymore. I keep it around for sentimental reasons."

A door slammed upstairs and Bert came running down the stairs, two by two. He stopped short when he saw J.P.

"What are you doing here?" he growled.

"I want to ask you some questions," said J.P., "about dognapping."

"You can't pin this rap on me," said Bert. "I don't know nothing about it. Besides I'd never touch anyone's mangy mutt."

"The dog was taken around five o'clock yesterday afternoon," said J.P. "Where were you about that time?"

"Right here," said Bert. He jerked his thumb towards the grandfather's clock. "It was three when I got home from school. I heard the clock bong six times when I left for the basketball game."

"You're lying," said J.P. "You're the dognapper and I can prove it."

"If you can, son," said Gus, "then I'll see that Bert is punished."

J.P. told Gus why Bert's story could not be true. Trapped, Bert broke down and admitted being the dognapper. J.P. left Bert in Gus's hands and went over to Jimmy's to check on Snookers.

How did J.P. know Bert was lying? Look for the clues and don't waste time closing this case.

Did you match wits with the famous detective?
Turn to page 47 and find out.

MINI MYSTERY SOLUTIONS

Mystery #1

R o h t a w n i o d
o t e h f l a r u a
d h a e t s l d t r
n a r p e a , s o k
e v d a r r o , n .
y e a r l e r a l
w s n k u n n n y
o e o r n o i d a
u e w i c c g c f
l n l g h t h o t
d o i h . u t m e
n r n t O r b e r

Mystery #2

T r r i a d x r x
h e d e d a , e l
e i *b* s f l t h e
c s *u* a i l h e f
l t *t* i n *b* e h t
u h . d i *u* r a t
e e J h s *t* e d o
h w a e h s f s d
e o m h e i o i o

Mystery #3

Inhis haste toble ndinw ithth eothe rstud ents, there dhead edboy andsh oplif tergr abbed abook andpr etend edtob eread ing.H ismis takew astha thewa shold ingth ebook upsid edown .Ther efore hecou ldnot haveb eenre ading foran hour.

Mystery #4

A	a	d	r	c	l	a	o	o
n	s	e	i	a	d	w	n	a
d	r	d	g	s	n	n	t	r
y	i	.	h	t	o	a	h	d
B	g	W	t	A	t	n	e	.
a	h	i	a	n	h	y	b	
r	t	t	r	d	a	t	l	
t	-	h	m	y	v	h	a	
e	h	h	i	c	e	i	c	
l	a	i	n	o	d	n	k	
w	n	s	a	u	r	g	b	

Mystery #5

```
A   ,   o   y   e   T   y   a   d   i   o
l   E   u   d   i   h   c   n   a   n   m
t   n   r   o   t   e   e   A   y   d   E
h   g   t   n   a   F   l   m   c   e   n
o   l   h   '   s   o   e   e   p   g
u   a   o   t   a   u   b   r   l   e   l
g   n   f   c   h   r   r   i   e   n   a
h   d   J   e   o   t   a   c   b   d   n
L   ,   u   l   l   h   t   a   r   e   d
o   h   l   e   i   o   i   n   a   n   .
n   a   y   b   d   f   o   h   t   c
d   s   t   r   a   J   n   o   i   e
o   a   h   a   y   u   i   l   n   f
n   f   e   t   .   l   s   i   g   r
```

Mystery #6

Sixt yeye smak esth irty bird sand
pupp ies. Bird shav etwo feet andp
uppi esha vefo urfe et.1 5×2= 30an
d15× 4=60 ,so6 0and 30eq ual9 0.Th
erea re15 bird sand 15pu ppie s.

Mystery #7

Ear lyi nth est ory wel ear ned
tha tAn nah ado nal ong blu esk
irt .Wi tha lon gsk irt itw oul dbe
imp oss ibl efo rAn nat ori dea boy
'sb ike tha tha sab ara cro sst hem
idd le.

Mystery #8

I	a	e	b	o	r	f	d	w	w	e
f	d	e	a	r	u	i	i	t	a	d
S	n	n	s	i	n	c	d	h	s	b
c	e	i	e	n	a	e	h	e	p	r
o	v	n	m	M	'	,	e	d	a	o
t	e	t	e	r	s	h	k	o	i	w
t	r	h	n	.	o	o	n	o	n	n
h	b	e	t	B	f	w	o	r	t	?

Mystery #9

Theba lloon mansa idhis heliu mtank
wasem ptyan dheha dtobl owthe ballo
onsup himse lf.Wi thnog asint hebal
loons andno toneb itofb reeze thatd
ay,th erewa snowa yabal loonc ouldh
avefl oated uptot hetre ebran ch.Th
erefo rethe jogge rwasl yingt oprot
ecthi mself .

Mystery #10

```
I  h  d  o  a  c  e  d  ,  v  i
f  a  t  t  s  a  y  b  n  e  t
G  d  h  s  h  r  w  e  o  r  h
r  u  e  t  t  ,  o  w  t  e  m
e  s  b  o  h  t  u  e  c  d  u
g  e  o  w  e  h  l  t  o  w  d
```

Mystery #11

```
A  a  o  t  d  t  n  e  o  s  e
d  l  z  t  e  i  e  .  r  w  l
o  w  e  e  n  o  y  T  e  e  v
z  a  n  r  o  n  y  h  t  r  e
e  y  n  w  m  o  o  e  h  i  .
n  s  o  h  i  f  u  r  e  s
i  a  m  a  n  m  u  e  a  t
s  d  a  t  a  o  s  f  n  w
```

Mystery #12

Terr yisa news pape rboy fort heMa
diso nMor ning Gaze tte. Ther efor
ehed eliv ersp aper sint hemo rnin
g,no tint heev enin gwhe nthe mech
anic sawt hene wsbo yste alin ghub
caps .Itc ould noth aveb eenT erry .

Mystery #13

I	o	n	t	r	e	g	b	e
f	l	o	o	o	m	e	e	c
y	d	t	a	r	e	w	q	l
o	t	e	m	,	s	i	u	e
u	h	u	i	t	s	l	i	a
h	e	p	r	h	a	l	t	r

Mystery #14

Bertma detwom istake s.One, heused
theter m"man gymutt "just ashedi
dinthe note.T wo,hes aidthe grandf
ather' sclock saidth reeo'c lockan
dbonge dsixti meswhe nhelef tforba
sketba ll.Imp ossibl e,sinc ethecl
ocksto ppedwo rkingt enyear sago.

Would you like to try and stump J.P.? Send him a letter with your favorite riddle or puzzle or even a mystery you think J.P. can't solve. He will answer every letter. Stump the Master and you will be awarded a certificate titling you Master Detective.

GOOD LUCK!

Send letters to:

J.P. Landers
c/o Childrens Press
1224 W. Van Buren St.
Chicago, Ill. 60607

About the Author

Marian Lee and her husband Ray live with their three children Greg 9, Lori, and Jeff 7 in Carson City, Nevada.

The author was born in Madison, Wisconsin and attended Wisconsin State University in Stevens Point and the University of Wisconsin in Milwaukee. In addition to writing J. P. Landers mysteries, the author's free time is devoted to reading, spending time with her children (who are her inspiration), and playing adventure games on her computer.

About the Artist

Steven Crombie was born in St. Paul, Minnesota. He received a first year scholarship award from the American Academy of Art in Chicago, Illinois. After graduation from the academy, Mr. Crombie worked as an assistant art director for a graphics company. He now does freelance illustration and design for advertising studios, publishers, and corporations in the Midwest.

A resident of Mount Prospect, Illinois, Steven's hobbies include skydiving and photography.